CW01064551

Darkness Rising

Andrew Lancaster and The Olympians, Volume 1

Tharun Vigneswar PS

Published by Tharun Vigneswar PS, 2024.

DARKNESS RISING

First edition. June 15, 2024.

Copyright © 2024 Tharun Vigneswar PS.

ISBN: 979-8224269549

Written by Tharun Vigneswar PS.

Table of Contents

Chapter 1

THE UNVEILING

The sunlight filtered through the towering skyscrapers of New York City, casting long shadows that danced across the bustling streets below. Andrew Lancaster sat alone in a quaint café nestled amidst the urban jungle, his mind lost in a labyrinth of swirling thoughts and unanswered questions.

It had started like any other day, with Andrew rising with the dawn and venturing out into the cacophony of the city. But as he made his way through the crowds of people, a peculiar sensation had settled over him—a feeling of being watched, of unseen eyes tracking his every move.

At first, Andrew had dismissed it as nothing more than paranoia, a side effect of living in a metropolis teeming with millions of souls. But as the feeling persisted, growing stronger with each passing moment, he couldn't shake the nagging suspicion that something was amiss.

And then, as he turned a corner and entered the café, he saw him—a figure lurking in the shadows, his presence as enigmatic as it was unsettling. Tall and imposing, with piercing blue eyes that seemed to penetrate the very depths of Andrew's soul, the stranger exuded an aura of quiet authority.

"Andrew Lancaster," the man said, his voice a low rumble that sent a shiver down Andrew's spine. "I've been searching for you."

Andrew blinked in surprise, his heart hammering in his chest. Who was this man, and how did he know his name? Before he could formulate a response, the stranger stepped forward, his gaze unwavering.

"My name is Michael Chip," he continued, his tone solemn. "And I come from a place called Camp Half-Blood."

Camp Half-Blood. The name sent a jolt of recognition through Andrew's mind, dredging up memories long buried beneath the sands of time. It was a name he had heard before, though he couldn't quite recall where or when.

"I've been sent to bring you there," Michael explained, his words laden with an unspoken urgency. "There's much we need to discuss, Andrew. Much you need to know."

And with that, Andrew's fate was sealed. Without a word, he rose from his seat and followed Michael out into the chaotic streets of the city, leaving behind the familiar comforts of the café and stepping into a world beyond his wildest imaginings.

As they walked, Michael spoke of gods and monsters, of heroes and legends—of a world that existed just beyond the veil of mortal perception. It was a world of danger and wonder, of adventure and intrigue—a world that Andrew could scarcely believe existed.

But with each passing moment, as they drew closer to their destination, Andrew's doubts began to fade, replaced by a sense of excitement and anticipation. For he knew that whatever lay ahead, it would be the beginning of an epic journey—one that would change the course of his life forever.

The streets of New York City buzzed with life as Andrew and Michael navigated their way through the bustling crowds. With each step, Andrew's mind raced with a whirlwind of thoughts and emotions, his heart pounding in his chest like a drumbeat echoing through the caverns of his soul.

As they walked, Michael continued to regale Andrew with tales of Camp Half-Blood, painting a vivid picture of a sanctuary hidden away from the prying eyes of mortals—a haven where demigods like Andrew could learn to harness their powers and fulfil their destinies.

"It's a place of refuge and training," Michael explained, his voice a steady anchor amidst the swirling chaos of the city. "A place where you can finally discover who you truly are, Andrew—a child of the gods."

Andrew listened intently, his mind whirling with a kaleidoscope of conflicting emotions. On one hand, there was a part of him that longed to embrace this newfound identity, to explore the depths of his divine heritage and unlock the mysteries of his existence. But on the other hand, there was a nagging voice of doubt—a voice that whispered tales of impossibility and disbelief, urging him to turn back and return to the safety of the world he had always known.

But deep down, Andrew knew that there was no turning back—that his destiny lay not in the familiar comforts of the mundane world, but in the uncharted territories of the supernatural realm. And so, with a resolve born of equal parts curiosity and determination, he pressed on, his footsteps echoing against the concrete jungle that surrounded them.

As they neared their destination, Andrew's senses were assailed by a cacophony of sights and sounds—a symphony of chaos that seemed to swirl and eddy around them like a stormy sea. But amidst the chaos, there was a sense of purpose—a guiding light that beckoned them forward with an irresistible allure.

And then, at long last, they arrived—a nondescript alleyway tucked away amidst the towering skyscrapers of the city, its entrance concealed from prying eyes by a veil of shadows and secrecy. It was here, in this hidden sanctuary, that the gates to Camp Half-Blood awaited them—a portal to a world beyond imagination, a world of gods and monsters, of heroes and legends.

With a sense of trepidation mingled with excitement, Andrew followed Michael into the alleyway, his heart racing with anticipation. And as they stepped through the gates and into the hallowed grounds of Camp Half-Blood, he knew that his life would never be the same again.

For here, amidst the towering pines and rolling hills of the camp, Andrew would embark on a journey of self-discovery and adventure—a journey that would test his courage and strength, his wit and wisdom, as he sought to uncover the truth of his own identity and forge his destiny in the fires of destiny.

And so, as the sun dipped below the horizon and cast its golden rays across the tranquil landscape, Andrew Lancaster stood at the threshold of a new beginning—a beginning filled with promise and possibility, with trials and tribulations, with triumphs and tragedies.

But one thing was certain—whatever lay ahead, Andrew would face it with bravery and determination born of the knowledge that he was not alone—that he had friends and allies by his side, and that together, they would overcome whatever challenges lay in their path.

The air within Camp Half-Blood was thick with anticipation as Andrew Lancaster and Michael Chip stepped through the gates, their arrival heralded by the rustling of leaves and the distant call of birdsong. The camp itself was a sprawling expanse of rugged wilderness, with clusters of cabins dotting the landscape like jewels scattered across a verdant tapestry.

As they made their way deeper into the heart of the camp, Andrew couldn't help but feel a sense of awe and wonder at the sights unfolding before him. Everywhere he looked, there were demigods training and sparring, their movements fluid and precise as they honed their skills under the watchful eye of their mentors.

"It's... it's incredible," Andrew breathed, his voice barely above a whisper as he took in the sights and sounds of his new surroundings.

Michael nodded, a small smile playing at the corners of his lips. "Welcome to Camp Half-Blood, Andrew—a haven for demigods like yourself, where you can finally learn to harness your powers and embrace your true destiny."

As they walked, Andrew couldn't help but notice the curious glances and whispered murmurs that followed in their wake. It was clear that news of his arrival had spread quickly throughout the camp, sparking a flurry of speculation and intrigue amongst the other campers.

But amidst the whispers and stares, there was also a sense of camaraderie—a shared bond that transcended the boundaries of age and experience. For here, amidst the towering pines and rolling hills of Camp Half-Blood, demigods of all shapes and sizes came together as one—a united front against the forces of darkness that lurked beyond the safety of the camp's borders.

And as Andrew looked around at the faces of his fellow campers, he knew that he had found a place where he truly belonged—a place where he could finally be himself, free from the constraints of the mortal world.

But even as he revelled in the warmth and acceptance of his newfound home, Andrew couldn't shake the nagging sense of unease that gnawed at the edges of his consciousness. For he knew that his journey was far from over—that the mysteries of his own identity still lay shrouded in shadow, waiting to be uncovered.

But with each passing moment, as he walked amidst the towering trees and whispered secrets of Camp Half-Blood, Andrew felt a flicker of hope—a glimmer of light amidst the darkness that threatened to engulf him. For here, amidst the warmth and camaraderie of his fellow demigods, he knew that he would find the answers he sought—that he would finally discover the truth of his destiny and embrace the hero that lay dormant within his soul.

And as he looked towards the horizon, where the setting sun bathed the landscape in a golden glow, Andrew knew that his adventure was only just beginning—that the trials and tribulations that lay ahead would only serve to strengthen his resolve and forge him into the hero he was destined to become.

As evening descended upon Camp Half-Blood, Andrew found himself standing before the imposing structure of the Hermes cabin—a temporary home for newcomers like himself, where they would stay until their divine parentage was officially determined. The cabin was a humble abode, its walls adorned with graffiti and memorabilia left behind by past occupants—a testament to the transient nature of life at camp.

With a sense of trepidation mingled with excitement, Andrew stepped through the threshold of the cabin, his footsteps echoing against the wooden floorboards. Inside, the cabin was a hive of activity, with demigods of all shapes and sizes milling about, their voices raised in animated conversation.

"Welcome to the Hermes cabin," a voice called out from the crowd, drawing Andrew's attention. Turning, he saw a young demigod with mischievous eyes and a crooked grin, his face lit up with the unmistakable glow of camaraderie. "I'm Jake, son of Hermes. And you must be the new kid, huh?"

Andrew nodded, returning Jake's smile with a tentative one of his own. "Yeah, that's me. Andrew Lancaster."

"Well, Andrew Lancaster, you've picked the right place to call home—at least for now," Jake said, clapping Andrew on the shoulder with a friendly gesture. "But hey, don't worry too much about it. Your divine parentage will be determined soon enough, and then you'll be off to your rightful cabin before you know it."

With a reassuring nod, Andrew settled into life at the Hermes cabin, his days filled with training and camaraderie as he awaited the fateful moment when his heritage would be revealed. But even as he immersed himself in the hustle and bustle of camp life, there was a part of him that couldn't shake the sense of anticipation that gnawed at the edges of his consciousness—a feeling that his destiny was on the brink of unfolding.

And then, one fateful evening, as Andrew sat down to dinner at the pavilion with his fellow campers, the air crackled with electric energy—a sense of anticipation that seemed to permeate the very fabric of the universe. For tonight was no ordinary night—tonight, a visitor of unparalleled importance would grace the camp with her presence.

As Andrew took his seat amongst the throngs of demigods, his heart raced with a mixture of excitement and apprehension. Who could it be that would warrant such a grand reception? And what could they possibly want with him, a mere newcomer to the world of gods and monsters?

But before he could dwell on these questions any longer, a hush fell over the pavilion as a figure stepped into the light—a figure so radiant and regal that Andrew felt a surge of awe wash over him like a tidal wave crashing against the shore.

It was Athena herself, the goddess of wisdom and warfare, her piercing grey eyes scanning the crowd with a gaze that seemed to pierce the very depths of their souls. And as she spoke, her voice was like music—a melodic blend of power and grace that sent shivers down Andrew's spine.

"Children of Olympus," Athena began, her voice resonating with a quiet authority that commanded the attention of all who heard it. "I have come to you tonight to claim one among you as my own—a child of my blood, destined for greatness."

As the campers held their breath in anticipation, Athena's gaze swept across the pavilion until it settled upon Andrew, her eyes alight with a spark of recognition. And in that moment, Andrew knew that his life would never be the same again—that he had been chosen by the goddess herself to walk a path of destiny and greatness.

With a sense of reverence and awe, Andrew rose to his feet, his heart pounding in his chest as he met Athena's gaze with unwavering determination, for he knew that this was only the beginning of his journey—that the road ahead would be fraught with danger and uncertainty, but also with adventure and triumph.

And as he stood before the goddess of wisdom and warfare, Andrew Lancaster knew that he was ready—for whatever challenges lay in store, whatever trials he would face. For he was no longer just a demigod—he was the son of Athena, destined for greatness beyond imagination. With Athena's guidance and wisdom to light his way, he would face the future with courage and resolve, ready to embrace whatever destiny had in store.

Chapter 2

THE QUEST BEGINS

As Andrew stood before Athena, his heart pounding with a mixture of awe and trepidation, the goddess of wisdom and warfare gazed down at him with eyes that seemed to pierce straight through to his soul. There was a gravity to her presence, a sense of ancient power that hummed in the air like an electric current.

"Andrew Lancaster," Athena spoke, her voice ringing clear and commanding across the pavilion. "You have been chosen by the gods for a great task—a quest of utmost importance that will test your courage, your wisdom, and your strength."

Andrew listened intently, his breath catching in his throat as he awaited the goddess's words. He knew that whatever task she had in store for him, it would be no small feat—not with Athena herself as his guide and mentor.

"I have chosen you to retrieve the Aegis—a powerful artefact that has been stolen from the halls of Olympus," Athena continued, her eyes blazing with righteous fury. "The Aegis can destroy immortals, and in the wrong hands, it poses a grave threat to both mortals and gods alike."

As Athena spoke, Andrew felt a chill run down his spine. The Aegis—a weapon of such incredible power that even the mightiest of gods would tremble at its sight. To think that such a weapon could fall into the hands of mortals was a thought too terrible to contemplate.

"But fear not, Andrew," Athena said, her voice softening slightly as she laid a gentle hand on his shoulder. "You will not face this task alone. You may choose two companions to accompany you on your quest, and together, you will journey to the ends of the earth to retrieve the Aegis and return it to its rightful place."

With a sense of determination burning in his chest, Andrew nodded solemnly, his mind already racing with the possibilities. But as he turned to face Chiron, the wise centaur who served as mentor to the camp's inhabitants, he knew that the choice of companions would not be an easy one.

"Chiron," Andrew said, addressing the centaur with a respectful nod. "I must choose two companions to accompany me on this quest. Who do you suggest?"

Chiron regarded Andrew with a knowing smile, his eyes twinkling with wisdom born of centuries of experience. "The choice is yours, Andrew. Choose those whom you trust, those whom you believe will stand by your side no matter what challenges may come."

With a nod of understanding, Andrew turned to face his fellow campers, his gaze sweeping across the pavilion until it settled upon two familiar faces—the satyr Michael Chip, whose guidance had led him to Camp Half-Blood in the first place, and Kiara Dean, daughter of Poseidon and his first friend at camp.

"Michael, Kiara," Andrew said, his voice firm with conviction. "Will you join me on this quest to retrieve the Aegis?"

Michael and Kiara exchanged a glance, their eyes shining with determination and resolve. "Of course, Andrew," Michael said, his voice steady and unwavering. "We'll be with you every step of the way."

And with that, the trio set off into the unknown, their hearts set on the task that lay ahead. They knew that the road ahead would be fraught with danger and uncertainty, but with courage and determination, they would overcome whatever challenges came their way.

With the weight of Athena's quest heavy on their shoulders, Andrew, Michael, and Kiara set out from Camp Half-Blood, their resolve steeled against the trials that lay ahead. The journey was arduous, fraught with peril and uncertainty, yet they pressed on with unwavering determination, their hearts set on the prize that awaited them at the end of their quest.

Their first destination was the Oracle of Delphi—a sacred sanctuary nestled amidst the craggy peaks of Mount Parnassus, where the wisdom of the gods was said to flow like a river of golden light. It was here, amidst the swirling mists and haunting echoes of prophecy, that they hoped to find guidance on their quest for the Aegis.

As they ascended the winding path that led to the oracle's cave, Andrew couldn't help but feel a sense of anticipation building within him—a thrill of excitement at the thought of what lay ahead. But beneath the surface, there also a nagging sense of unease—a feeling that their journey was far from over and that the challenges they faced would only grow more daunting with each passing moment.

But Andrew pushed aside his doubts, focusing instead on the task at hand. For he knew that the fate of Camp Half-Blood—and perhaps even the world itself—hung in the balance, and that failure was not an option.

At long last, they reached the entrance to the oracle's cave—a yawning abyss shrouded in darkness and mystery. With a deep breath, Andrew stepped forward, his heart pounding in his chest as he braced himself for what lay ahead.

As they entered the cave, they were met with a scene straight out of legend—a chamber bathed in the soft glow of flickering torchlight, its walls adorned with ancient runes and symbols of power. And at the centre of it all stood the oracle herself—a figure cloaked in shadow, her face hidden beneath a veil of mystery.

As Andrew stood before the oracle, a torrent of questions raced through his mind, each one more pressing than the last. But foremost among them was the burning inquiry that had driven him to seek out the oracle's guidance in the first place—the whereabouts of the Aegis, the powerful artefact they had been tasked with retrieving.

"Oracle," Andrew began, his voice steady despite the nervous flutter in his chest. "We seek the Aegis, a weapon of great power. Can you tell us where it may be found?"

The oracle regarded Andrew with eyes that seemed to pierce straight through to his soul, her expression inscrutable beneath the veil of shadow that shrouded her face. And then, with a voice like the whisper of the wind through ancient ruins, she spoke.

"The Aegis lies hidden within the heart of the labyrinth," the oracle intoned, her words carrying the weight of centuries of prophecy and foresight. "There, it waits for those with the courage and strength to claim it. But beware, for the guardians of the labyrinth are fierce and unyielding, and only those who are worthy may pass."

Andrew's heart skipped a beat at the oracle's words, the gravity of their task settling over him like a heavy cloak. The labyrinth—a place of mystery and danger, where legends were born and heroes were forged. It would be their greatest challenge yet, but he knew that they had no choice but to press on.

But just as Andrew was about to speak, the oracle's voice rang out once more, her words carrying an unexpected twist.

"And beyond the Aegis, another task awaits," she continued, her tone taking on a solemn note. "Two new demigods shall cross your path, their destinies intertwined with yours. One born of fire and steel, the other of darkness and shadow. Together, they shall play a pivotal role in the fate of Olympus."

Andrew exchanged a bewildered glance with Michael and Kiara, their minds racing to comprehend the oracle's cryptic words. Two new demigods—born of fire and steel, darkness and shadow. What role would they play in their quest for the Aegis, and how would their destinies intertwine with their own?

But there was no time to dwell on the oracle's prophecy, for their journey awaited them, and the fate of Camp Half-Blood hung in the balance. With a sense of determination burning in his chest, Andrew turned to his companions, his gaze steady and unwavering.

"We have our task, my friends," he said, his voice ringing with resolve. "Let us venture forth into the labyrinth and retrieve the Aegis, whatever the cost. And when the time comes, we will face whatever challenges lie ahead, together."

And with that, Andrew, Michael, and Kiara set out from the oracle's cave, their hearts set on the path that lay ahead, and the destiny that awaited them at the heart of the labyrinth.

As they ventured forth from the oracle's cave, the words of the prophecy echoed in their minds, guiding their steps and fueling their determination. The labyrinth awaited them—a twisting maze of corridors and chambers, where danger lurked around every corner and mysteries lay hidden in the shadows.

As Andrew, Michael, and Kiara made their way through the bustling streets of New York City towards Central Park, their senses were on high alert, keenly aware of the dangers that lurked in the shadows. The city buzzed with life around them, oblivious to the supernatural threats that lay just beyond mortal perception.

Suddenly, a deafening roar shattered the tranquillity of the urban landscape, sending a shiver down Andrew's spine. Without hesitation, he drew his sword, his muscles tensing in anticipation as he scanned the surroundings for the source of the disturbance.

Emerging from the shadows of an alleyway, a monstrous figure lumbered into view—a towering beast with claws as sharp as daggers and eyes that glowed with malevolent intent. It was a chimera, a fearsome creature born of fire and fury, and it hungered for blood.

As the monstrous chimera's roar shattered the tranquillity of Central Park, Andrew, Michael, and Kiara swiftly assumed defensive stances, preparing for the inevitable clash.

Just as the chimera lunged forward, its claws poised to strike, a figure dashed into view, wielding a weapon with practised ease. Andrew's attention was momentarily diverted by the newcomer, whose arrival seemed almost too fortuitous to be a mere coincidence. Yet, in the chaos of the moment, there was little time for contemplation.

With instincts honed by training and adrenaline, Andrew moved to engage the chimera alongside Michael and Kiara, their coordinated efforts driving the beast back. As the battle raged on, the newcomer's actions proved instrumental in turning the tide, his skill and determination evident in every strike.

After a fierce struggle, the chimera was finally subdued, its roars fading into defeated whimpers as it collapsed to the ground. As the dust settled, Andrew turned to acknowledge their unexpected ally, his curiosity piqued by the stranger's presence.

"Thank you for your assistance," Andrew said, his voice carrying genuine gratitude. "You fought bravely."

The newcomer offered a nod of acknowledgement, his expression masked by the shadows of the park. Though Andrew couldn't discern much about him in the dim light, he couldn't shake the feeling that there was more to this stranger than met the eye.

As the chaos of battle subsided and the chimera lay defeated at their feet, the stranger stepped forward, his features illuminated by the soft glow of the park's lamplight. With a hesitant yet determined stride, he approached Andrew, Michael, and Kiara, his expression a mixture of relief and apprehension.

"I owe you my thanks," he began, his voice tinged with a hint of gratitude. "I couldn't have taken down that beast on my own."

Andrew regarded the newcomer with a mixture of curiosity and wariness, his mind racing with questions. Who was this lone demigod, and what had led him to Central Park on this fateful night? With the chimera vanquished and the immediate threat neutralized, Andrew saw an opportunity to learn more about their unexpected ally.

"What's your name?" Andrew inquired, his tone measured yet friendly. "And what brings you to Central Park at this hour?"

The demigod hesitated for a moment as if weighing his response carefully before speaking. "My name is Adrian McCall," he revealed, his voice steady despite the uncertainty that lingered in his eyes. "I'm a son of Hephaestus, and I've been travelling alone for some time now, seeking... answers."

Andrew's eyebrows raised in surprise at the revelation. A fellow demigod, and a son of Hephaestus no less. It was a rare encounter indeed, and one that held the promise of new alliances and shared purpose.

"Well, Adrian," Andrew said, offering a warm smile. "We're on a quest of our own—to find the Aegis and protect Camp Half-Blood from a looming threat. If you're willing, we could use your help."

Adrian's eyes sparkled with a mixture of determination and curiosity, his resolve firming as he considered Andrew's offer. "I may not know much about your quest," he admitted, "but I'm more than willing to lend a hand. Together, we stand a better chance of facing whatever challenges lie ahead."

With a shared nod of agreement, Andrew, Michael, Kiara, and Adrian set off once more, their footsteps echoing through the silent streets of Central Park as they ventured forth into the darkness.

As the dust settled and the adrenaline of battle began to wane, Andrew couldn't shake the feeling that there was something significant about the stranger who had come to their aid. As they exchanged brief introductions, Andrew's mind raced with the possibilities, trying to piece together the puzzle of their unexpected ally's identity.

Adrian McCall, son of Hephaestus—the name echoed in Andrew's mind, resonating with a sense of familiarity that he couldn't quite place. It was as if a piece of the puzzle had clicked into place, connecting the dots of the prophecy that had guided their quest thus far.

Could it be that Adrian was one of the demigods mentioned in the oracle's prophecy—the one born of fire and steel, destined to play a pivotal role in their journey? The thought sent a shiver down Andrew's spine, filling him with a renewed sense of purpose and determination.

As they continued on their journey, Andrew found himself observing Adrian with newfound curiosity, searching for clues that might confirm his suspicions. Though the demigod remained somewhat enigmatic about his past and motivations, there was an undeniable sense of camaraderie that began to form between them—a shared sense of purpose that transcended the boundaries of their individual quests.

With each step they took, Andrew felt a sense of anticipation building within him, a feeling that they were drawing closer to the truth that lay at the heart of their journey. And as they ventured forth into the unknown, he knew that whatever challenges lay ahead, they would face them together—as allies, as friends, and perhaps, as the heroes foretold in the prophecy that had brought them together.

Chapter 3

TWIST OF FATE

The labyrinth stretched out before them like a tangled web of shadows and secrets, its twisting corridors shrouded in darkness and mystery. As Andrew, Michael, Kiara, and Adrian ventured deeper into its depths, they remained ever vigilant, their senses alert to the slightest hint of danger.

It was amidst the labyrinth's winding passages that their journey took an unexpected turn. From the darkness emerged a lone figure, his silhouette obscured by the shifting shadows. Before any of them could react, the stranger lunged forward, his movements swift and precise as he launched into an attack.

Caught off guard by the sudden assault, Andrew and his companions sprang into action, their weapons at the ready as they sought to defend themselves against their mysterious assailant. Blades clashed and spells crackled in the air as the confrontation escalated, each side locked in a desperate struggle for survival.

Amid the chaos, Andrew's mind raced, trying to make sense of the situation. Who was this stranger, and why had he attacked them without provocation? As the battle raged on, Andrew couldn't shake the feeling that there was more to this encounter than met the eye.

With a quick motion of his hand, Andrew signalled for his companions to hold their fire, his voice cutting through the cacophony of combat with calm authority.

"Stop!" he commanded, his tone firm yet measured. "This fighting serves no purpose. We must hear him out."

As his companions reluctantly lowered their weapons, Andrew approached the stranger cautiously, his eyes never leaving the man's face. There was something familiar about him, something that stirred a memory deep within Andrew's mind, but try as he might, he couldn't quite place it.

"Why did you attack us?" Andrew asked, his voice tinged with curiosity and caution.

The stranger regarded Andrew with a mixture of defiance and uncertainty, his gaze flickering between the members of the group as if weighing his options. And then, with a sigh of resignation, he lowered his weapon, the tension in his shoulders easing slightly as he spoke.

"I'm sorry," he said, his voice tinged with remorse. "I thought... I thought you were someone else."

As the adrenaline of battle began to ebb away, the stranger introduced himself as Harry Fletcher—a lost soul adrift in the labyrinth of fate, haunted by shadows of his own past. Though he remained guarded and wary, there was a vulnerability in his eyes that spoke of a deeper pain—a pain that Andrew couldn't help but empathize with.

With a sense of understanding and compassion, Andrew offered Harry a place among their group, extending a hand of friendship in the face of uncertainty and doubt. And as Harry reluctantly accepted, a bond began to form between them—a bond forged in the crucible of adversity, tempered by the trials of their shared journey.

With Harry now a part of their group, Andrew and his companions pressed on into the labyrinth's depths, their footsteps echoing through the darkness as they ventured forth into the unknown. For in the labyrinth of fate, where twists and turns awaited at every corner, they had found something far more precious than any treasure or artefact—they had found each other.

As they ventured deeper into the labyrinth, the group's dynamic shifted, with Harry's presence adding both tension and a sense of mystery to their journey. Despite Andrew's offer of friendship, Harry remained guarded, his eyes constantly scanning their surroundings as if expecting danger at every turn.

The tension reached a boiling point one evening as they made camp in a secluded alcove of the labyrinth. Andrew, ever the peacemaker, attempted to ease the atmosphere with light conversation, but Harry's brooding silence only seemed to exacerbate the unease that hung in the air.

Sensing the growing tension, Adrian attempted to lighten the mood with a jest, but his efforts fell flat in the face of Harry's stoic demeanour. Michael, always quick to diffuse conflict, attempted to steer the conversation towards their shared goal—the quest for the Aegis—but even that seemed to do little to quell the palpable tension that simmered beneath the surface.

Finally, unable to bear the tension any longer, Harry rose to his feet, his expression dark and unreadable as he addressed the group. "I didn't ask to be here," he began, his voice tinged with bitterness. "I have my own reasons for seeking the Aegis, and they have nothing to do with any of you."

Andrew, ever the diplomat, attempted to reason with Harry, urging him to put aside his differences and work together towards their common goal. But Harry's stubbornness remained unyielding, his resolve unwavering in the face of Andrew's attempts at reconciliation.

As the argument escalated, emotions ran high, with accusations and grievances exchanged in a flurry of heated words. And then, in a moment of frustration and anger, Harry lashed out, his fists clenched in a display of defiance that threatened to escalate into violence.

But before the situation could escalate further, Andrew stepped forward, his voice calm yet commanding as he sought to defuse the tension that hung in the air. With words of understanding and empathy, he reminded the group of the importance of unity and cooperation, urging them to set aside their differences in the face of the challenges that lay ahead.

Moved by Andrew's words, the group gradually began to lower their defences, their animosity giving way to a sense of solidarity and camaraderie. And as they sat beneath the canopy of stars, the weight of their shared purpose hanging heavy in the air, they knew that they had overcome yet another obstacle on their journey towards the Aegis.

With the rift between them mended, Andrew, Michael, Kiara, Adrian, and Harry settled down for the night, their hearts united in purpose as they prepared to face whatever challenges awaited them in the labyrinth's treacherous depths. For in the crucible of adversity, they had forged a bond that would carry them through the darkest of times—a bond that would see them through to the end of their quest, no matter what trials lay in store.

As the night deepened and the stars sparkled overhead, the group found themselves drawn into a conversation that delved into the depths of their pasts and their divine parentage.

Andrew, ever the strategist and seeker of knowledge, took the lead, sharing his experiences as a son of Athena. He spoke of his childhood spent navigating the complexities of mortal life, his mind always hungry for knowledge and his heart yearning for a sense of belonging. He recounted the day Michael Chip, the wise and caring satyr, had found him and brought him to Camp Half-Blood—a moment that had forever changed the course of his destiny.

Kiara, daughter of Poseidon, shared her own story next, her voice soft yet tinged with an undeniable strength born of years spent honing her skills as a demigod. She spoke of her upbringing at camp, her days spent training in the ways of the sea, and the friendships she had forged along the way. Despite the challenges she had faced, Kiara's spirit remained unbroken, her determination to protect those she cared about shining through in every word she spoke.

Adrian, the son of Hephaestus, offered a glimpse into his own past—a past marked by hardship and struggle, yet tempered by the fires of his own determination. He spoke of his time wandering alone in the wilderness, his hands skilled in the art of crafting weapons and tools that would aid him in his quest for purpose and redemption. And though his path had been fraught with obstacles, Adrian's resolve remained unshakable, his belief in the power of creation and innovation serving as a guiding light in the darkness.

Finally, it was Harry's turn to share his story—a story marked by tragedy and loss, yet tempered by a fierce determination to seek justice for those he had lost. With a heavy heart, he spoke of his brother, Marcus Fletcher, a demigod whose life had been cut short by unknown assailants within the labyrinth's treacherous depths.

Harry's voice trembled with emotion as he recounted the events that had led him to this moment—a moment where he stood on the precipice of a journey that would lead him to the truth behind his brother's death and the justice he sought to uphold in his memory.

As the group listened to Harry's tale, their hearts heavy with empathy and understanding, a sense of solidarity washed over them—a shared understanding of the burdens they each carried, and the strength they found in one another's company. And as they settled in for the night, their bonds stronger than ever, they knew that whatever trials lay ahead, they would face them together—as allies, as friends, and as champions of a destiny that had yet to unfold.

As the night slowly surrendered to the gentle embrace of dawn, a soft golden glow began to spread across the horizon, painting the sky in hues of pink and orange. The darkness that had shrouded the labyrinth's depths began to recede, replaced by the warm embrace of the morning sun.

With the coming of the new day, a sense of hope and renewal washed over the group—a feeling that anything was possible, and that with each sunrise came the promise of a fresh start.

Andrew, ever the strategist, took stock of their surroundings, his mind already turning towards the challenges that lay ahead. With a sense of purpose and determination, he began to outline their plan for the day, his words infused with the quiet confidence of a leader who knew that victory lay within their grasp.

Michael, the wise and caring satyr, offered words of encouragement and support, his presence a reassuring presence amidst the uncertainty of their journey. With a gentle smile, he reminded the group of the strength they found in one another's company and the bonds that held them together through even the darkest of times.

Kiara, daughter of Poseidon, stood tall and resolute, her eyes sparkling with determination as she prepared to face whatever challenges awaited them in the labyrinth's treacherous depths. With a nod of affirmation, she pledged her unwavering loyalty to the group, her spirit undaunted by the trials that lay ahead.

Adrian, the son of Hephaestus, busied himself with preparations for the day ahead, his hands deftly crafting tools and weapons that would aid them in their quest. With each stroke of his hammer, he infused his creations with the strength of his own determination, a testament to his unwavering commitment to their shared cause.

And Harry, the newest member of their group, watched silently from the sidelines, his eyes reflecting a mixture of uncertainty and determination. Though the shadows of his past still lingered in the corners of his mind, there was a glimmer of hope in his gaze—a hope born of the newfound camaraderie he had found amongst his companions.

As the sun rose higher in the sky, casting its warm rays upon the labyrinth's ancient walls, the group set out once more on their journey, their hearts united in purpose as they ventured forth into the unknown. For in the light of a new day, they knew that anything was possible—that with courage, determination, and the strength of their bond, they could overcome any obstacle that stood in their way.

And so, with heads held high and spirits soaring, Andrew, Michael, Kiara, Adrian, and Harry pressed on, their footsteps echoing through the labyrinth's corridors as they chased the promise of a destiny that awaited them just beyond the horizon. For in the light of the rising sun, they knew that their greatest adventure had only just begun.

Chapter 4

BONDS OF FRIENDSHIP

As the days turned into weeks and the journey through the labyrinth stretched on, Andrew, Kiara, Adrian, Harry, and Michael Chip found themselves drawn together by the bonds of friendship forged in the crucible of adversity.

Despite their differences, they stood united in their quest for the Aegis, their shared purpose serving as a beacon of hope amidst the darkness that surrounded them. With each passing day, their trust in one another grew stronger, their spirits buoyed by the knowledge that they were not alone in their struggles.

It was during their moments of respite, as they rested beneath the shade of ancient trees or huddled around crackling campfires, that Kiara shared stories of her childhood at Camp Half-Blood. She spoke of the trials and triumphs she had faced as a demigod, the friendships she had forged, and the bonds that had sustained her through even the darkest of times.

Her words painted a vivid picture of life within the walls of the camp—the camaraderie shared between campers, the thrill of training and competition, and the sense of belonging that came from being surrounded by others who understood the challenges of being a demigod.

As Andrew, Adrian, Harry, and Michael listened to Kiara's stories, their hearts swelled with admiration for the strength and resilience she had shown in the face of adversity. Her tales served as a reminder of the power of friendship, and the importance of standing together in times of need.

But their newfound camaraderie would soon be put to the test, as betrayal and danger lurked around every corner of the labyrinth. Shadows of the past resurfaced, old wounds reopened, and the bonds that held them together threatened to unravel in the face of betrayal.

As tensions rose and loyalties were tested, Andrew, Kiara, Adrian, Harry, and Michael found themselves facing their greatest challenge yet—a challenge that would put their friendship, their courage, and their determination to the ultimate test.

As the group pressed deeper into the labyrinth, the oppressive darkness seemed to close in around them, the air thick with a sense of foreboding. The ground trembled beneath their feet with each step, a tangible sign of the formidable adversary they were about to face.

Antaeus, the towering giant, loomed before them like a living mountain, his massive form wreathed in shadows as he prepared to unleash his fury upon the unsuspecting intruders. His eyes burned with a fierce intensity, his muscles coiled like springs as he awaited the inevitable clash.

Andrew, Kiara, Adrian, Harry, and Michael Chip exchanged wary glances, their hearts pounding in their chests as they braced themselves for battle. Despite their fears, they stood united in their resolve, their determination unyielding in the face of overwhelming odds.

With a roar that echoed through the labyrinth's twisting corridors, Antaeus launched himself forward, his fists swinging in a deadly arc as he unleashed a barrage of blows upon his adversaries.

The ground shook with each thunderous impact, sending shockwaves rippling through the air as the group fought desperately to defend themselves against the relentless assault.

Blades clashed and spells crackled in the air as the group unleashed their full arsenal of skills and abilities, each member contributing to the fray with their own unique talents. Andrew's strategic mind guided their movements, his keen instincts helping to anticipate Antaeus's next move. Kiara's mastery of water and sea granted her agility and precision in combat, her attacks laced with the fury of the ocean's wrath. Adrian's craftsmanship proved invaluable, his inventions and creations providing crucial support in their battle against the giant.

But despite their best efforts, Antaeus proved to be a formidable opponent, his strength seemingly endless as he shrugged off blow after blow with ease. With each passing moment, the group's resolve began to waver, their energy waning as they struggled to keep pace with the relentless onslaught of their adversary.

It was then, in the heat of battle, that Harry unleashed a power unlike anything they had ever seen before—a surge of dark energy that crackled in the air as he summoned forth spirits from the depths of the underworld. With a mighty roar, he commanded the spirits to bind Antaeus, trapping the giant in a web of ethereal chains that rendered him powerless to resist.

As the dust settled and the echoes of battle faded into silence, Andrew's eyes widened in realization as he beheld Harry's newfound power—a power that could only belong to one of Hades' own. With a sense of awe and understanding, he recognized Harry as the second demigod mentioned in the prophecy, the one born of darkness and death, destined to play a pivotal role in their journey.

With Antaeus defeated and Harry's true identity revealed, the group stood victorious amidst the wreckage of their battle, their hearts filled with a newfound sense of purpose and determination. For in that moment, they knew that they had overcome yet another obstacle on their journey—a journey that would lead them ever closer to the truth behind the Aegis and the destiny that awaited them at its end.

As Harry revealed the tragic story of his brother's demise, Andrew's heart swelled with empathy and determination. He could feel the weight of Harry's burden pressing down upon them both, a heavy mantle of grief and vengeance that threatened to consume them.

"Harry," Andrew said, his voice filled with resolve, "you don't have to face this alone. I'll help you find the answers you seek, and together, we'll bring those responsible for your brother's death to justice."

Harry's eyes flickered with a mixture of gratitude and determination as he nodded in agreement. "Thank you, Andrew," he said, his voice tinged with emotion. "I couldn't do this without you."

As they stood together amidst the labyrinth's ancient walls, Andrew felt a renewed sense of purpose coursing through his veins. Together, he and Harry would unravel the mysteries of the labyrinth, uncover the truth behind Marcus Fletcher's murder, and ensure that justice was served.

But as Harry spoke of Antaeus and the symbol he had seen upon the giant's banner, Andrew's thoughts turned to the implications of their encounter. Could it be possible that Antaeus was somehow connected to Marcus's death? And if so, what secrets did the labyrinth hold that could shed light on this dark and twisted puzzle?

With a sense of urgency burning in his chest, Andrew turned to Harry, his eyes alight with determination. "We need to find out more about this symbol," he said, his voice firm. "If it's connected to Marcus's death, then we need to uncover the truth behind it. And I won't rest until we do."

Together, Andrew and Harry vowed to delve deeper into the labyrinth, to seek out the answers they so desperately sought, and to bring justice to those who had wronged them. For in the labyrinth of fate, where secrets lurked around every corner and danger lurked in the shadows, they knew that their bond of friendship would be their greatest strength—a guiding light in the darkness, leading them ever closer to the truth.

One evening, as they made camp in a secluded alcove of the labyrinth, Harry approached the group with a determined look in his eyes. He knew that the time had come to reveal the truth about his identity, to lay bare the secrets that he had kept hidden for so long.

"Everyone," Harry began, his voice steady yet tinged with emotion, "there's something I need to tell you. Something that I should have shared with you from the beginning."

As the group turned their attention towards him, their expressions a mixture of curiosity and concern, Harry took a deep breath and began to speak.

"My name is Harry Fletcher," he said, his voice carrying the weight of years of secrecy and solitude. "I am a son of Hades, and the brother of Marcus Fletcher—the demigod whose death I have been seeking to avenge."

As Harry's words hung in the air, the group's reactions varied—some looked on with shock, others with understanding, but all with a sense of unwavering support. Andrew, Kiara, Adrian, and Michael Chip listened intently as Harry recounted the story of his past, the tragedies he had endured, and the journey that had brought him to this moment.

"I understand if this changes things between us," Harry said, his voice tinged with uncertainty. "But I couldn't continue to hide who I am, not from the people I've come to trust and respect."

But to Harry's surprise and relief, the group's response was one of unwavering solidarity and support. Andrew clasped Harry's shoulder in a gesture of camaraderie, a silent acknowledgement of the bond that now bound them together.

"We're a team, Harry," Andrew said, his voice filled with conviction. "And that means we stand by each other, no matter what. Your past doesn't define you—it's what you do with it that matters. And from what I've seen, you're a true hero in every sense of the word."

With a sense of relief flooding through him, Harry felt a weight lift from his shoulders—a weight that he had carried for far too long. And as they settled in for the night, their hearts lightened by the knowledge that they stood united as friends and allies, Harry knew that he had finally found his place amongst them.

Chapter 5

THE TRIALS OF THE LABYRINTH

As the group delved deeper into the heart of the treacherous labyrinth, they found themselves faced with a series of daunting trials that tested their strength, courage, and wit.

Each twist and turn of the labyrinth brought with it new challenges—deadly traps, cunning puzzles, and hidden dangers lurking in the shadows. But with Adrian's engineering skills and Andrew's strategic mind leading the way, they tackled each obstacle with determination and ingenuity, inching ever closer to their goal.

Their journey through the labyrinth was fraught with peril, but it was also marked by moments of triumph and camaraderie. Together, they navigated twisting corridors and perilous chasms, their bond of friendship growing stronger with each passing trial.

At one point, they found themselves confronted by a maze of shifting walls and hidden passages, its intricate design seemingly designed to confound and confuse. But with Adrian's keen eye for detail and Andrew's strategic acumen, they managed to map out a path through the maze, avoiding the deadly traps that lay in wait at every turn.

In another trial, they were forced to confront a series of riddles and puzzles that guarded the entrance to a hidden chamber deep within the labyrinth. With Kiara's knowledge of ancient lore and Harry's intuitive understanding of the arcane, they deciphered each puzzle with ease, unlocking the secrets that lay buried within.

But perhaps their greatest challenge came in the form of a labyrinthine maze that stretched out before them like a tangled web of confusion and deception. With no clear path forward, they were forced to rely on their instincts and intuition, trusting in each other to guide them through the darkness.

Despite the dangers that lurked around every corner, the group pressed on with unwavering determination, their spirits buoyed by the knowledge that they were not alone in their struggles. And as they faced each trial together, they grew ever closer as friends and allies, bound by a shared purpose and a common goal.

As the group stood in the chamber, their eyes fixed on the pedestal where the Aegis should have rested, a sense of disbelief washed over them. The pedestal lay empty, devoid of the powerful artefact they had risked so much to find.

Confusion and frustration clouded their minds as they searched the chamber for any sign of the Aegis. But despite their best efforts, the artefact remained elusive, its whereabouts shrouded in mystery.

"We must have missed something," Adrian muttered, his brow furrowed in concentration as he scanned the chamber for any hidden compartments or secret passages.

Kiara clenched her fists in frustration, her eyes scanning the room with a sense of determination. "There has to be a clue somewhere," she said, her voice tinged with frustration. "We can't give up now."

Andrew's mind raced as he tried to make sense of their situation. Had they been led astray? Was the Aegis merely a myth, a figment of their imagination?

But before he could voice his doubts, a voice echoed through the chamber—a whisper on the edge of perception, barely audible yet filled with undeniable urgency.

"The Aegis lies not in this chamber, but beyond it," the voice intoned, its words sending a shiver down Andrew's spine. "To find it, you must first prove yourselves worthy."

With a sense of determination burning in their hearts, the group pressed on, their resolve strengthened by the knowledge that their quest was far from over. For in the labyrinth of fate, where secrets lurked around every corner and danger lurked in the shadows, they knew that their journey was far from over.

As they ventured deeper into the labyrinth, the air grew thick with tension, and a palpable sense of foreboding hung heavy in the air. Every step they took seemed to lead them further into the labyrinth's twisting maze of shadows and secrets, each turn revealing new challenges and dangers.

The walls of the labyrinth seemed to close in around them, the darkness pressing in from all sides as if seeking to swallow them whole. But despite the oppressive atmosphere, the group pressed on, their determination unshaken by the trials that lay ahead.

With each passing moment, the labyrinth seemed to grow more treacherous, its passages filled with traps and pitfalls designed to ensnare the unwary. But with Adrian's engineering prowess and Andrew's strategic acumen leading the way, they navigated the labyrinth's intricate pathways with skill and precision, sidestepping danger at every turn.

But as they delved deeper into the labyrinth's depths, they encountered challenges that tested not only their physical prowess but their mental fortitude as well. Riddles and puzzles lay in their path, each one more fiendish than the last, forcing them to rely on their wits and intellect to unravel the mysteries that lay before them.

Yet despite the odds stacked against them, the group pressed on, their determination unwavering in the face of adversity. With each challenge they overcame, they grew stronger, their bond of friendship forged ever deeper by the trials they faced together.

But as they journeyed deeper into the labyrinth, they could sense that they were drawing closer to their goal. The air crackled with a sense of anticipation, and a faint glimmer of light beckoned to them from the depths of the labyrinth's darkness—a beacon of hope amidst the shadows that surrounded them.

Their first skirmish came unexpectedly, as they rounded a corner and found themselves face to face with a pack of snarling hellhounds, their eyes gleaming with malice as they lunged forward with razor-sharp teeth bared. With a fierce battle cry, Andrew leapt into action, his sword flashing in the dim light as he fended off the ferocious beasts with skilful strikes and well-timed parries. Kiara called upon the power of the sea, conjuring waves of water to douse the flames that licked at the hellhounds' fur, while Adrian unleashed a barrage of mechanical traps to ensnare their foes.

But the hellhounds were only the beginning, as they soon found themselves confronted by even more formidable adversaries. A towering chimera emerged from the darkness, its lion's roar echoing through the labyrinth as it charged forward with claws extended and jaws agape. Harry summoned forth shadows to cloak their movements, while Michael Chip darted in and out of the creature's reach, his hooves pounding against the stone floor as he harried their foe from behind.

Yet despite their valiant efforts, the chimera proved to be a formidable opponent, its strength and ferocity unmatched by any foe they had faced thus far. With each swipe of its claws and snap of its jaws, it pushed them to the brink of exhaustion, testing their skills and resolve in a battle that seemed destined to end in tragedy.

But just when all seemed lost, a glimmer of hope appeared on the horizon—a blinding flash of light that illuminated the darkness and sent the chimera reeling back in surprise. With a triumphant cry, Andrew seized the opportunity, driving his sword deep into the creature's heart and vanquishing it once and for all.

As the dust settled and the echoes of battle faded into silence, the group stood victorious amidst the wreckage of their fallen foe, their chests heaving with exertion and their spirits uplifted by the knowledge that they had emerged triumphant in the face of overwhelming odds. For in the labyrinth of fate, where danger lurked around every corner and monsters prowled in the shadows, they knew that their bond of friendship would be their greatest strength—a beacon of hope in the darkness, guiding them towards the light of a brighter tomorrow.

Chapter 6

FACING THE MINOTAUR

In the depths of the labyrinth, the group faced their greatest challenge yet: a fierce battle with the legendary Minotaur. As they ventured deeper into the maze-like corridors, the air grew thick with tension, and a sense of foreboding settled over them like a shroud.

Andrew, Kiara, Adrian, Harry, and Michael Chip knew that they had to be prepared for anything as they pressed forward, their senses heightened and their weapons at the ready. They had faced countless trials and adversaries in their journey through the labyrinth, but none compared to the fearsome reputation of the Minotaur—a monstrous creature with the body of a man and the head of a bull, said to be the guardian of the labyrinth's darkest depths.

With Andrew's leadership guiding them, the group moved cautiously through the labyrinth, their footsteps echoing off the ancient stone walls as they searched for signs of their elusive quarry. Every shadow seemed to conceal a potential threat, and every corner held the promise of danger.

Suddenly, a low growl echoed through the corridors, sending a shiver down their spines. They knew that they had found what they were looking for—the Minotaur was near.

As they rounded a corner, their worst fears were realized as they came face to face with the monstrous beast. Towering over them, its massive form seemed to fill the entire corridor, its eyes glowing with a fierce intensity as it prepared to charge.

But Andrew was undeterred. Drawing his sword with a steely determination, he stepped forward to face the Minotaur head-on, his gaze never wavering from the creature's fearsome visage.

"We can do this," he said, his voice firm and resolute. "Together, we can defeat the Minotaur and continue our quest."

With Kiara's mastery of water and Harry's control over shadows, they devised a plan to outwit the monstrous beast. Kiara summoned forth waves of water to slow the Minotaur's movements, while Harry cloaked the group in shadows to conceal their approach.

As the Minotaur charged forward with a deafening roar, Adrian sprang into action, unleashing a barrage of mechanical traps to ensnare the creature's legs and immobilize it. With the Minotaur momentarily distracted, Andrew seized the opportunity to strike, driving his sword deep into the creature's side with a mighty blow.

But the Minotaur was not so easily defeated. With a furious bellow, it lashed out with its massive horns, sending Andrew sprawling to the ground. But before the creature could deliver the killing blow, Kiara stepped forward, her eyes blazing with determination as she summoned forth a torrent of water to engulf the Minotaur in a swirling vortex.

As the creature thrashed and roared in the grip of Kiara's watery embrace, Harry seized the opportunity to strike, his shadows coalescing into tendrils of darkness that ensnared the Minotaur's limbs and held it fast.

With the creature immobilized, Adrian and Michael Chip moved in to deliver the final blow, their weapons striking true as they drove the Minotaur to the ground with a resounding thud.

As the dust settled and the echoes of battle faded into silence, the group stood victorious amidst the wreckage of their fallen foe, their chests heaving with exertion and their spirits uplifted by the knowledge that they had emerged triumphant in the face of overwhelming odds.

But as they caught their breath and tended to their wounds, they knew that their journey through the labyrinth was far from over. For in the heart of the maze, where secrets lurked around every corner and dangers abounded, they knew that their greatest challenges still lay ahead. And with their courage and determination as their guide, they pressed on, ready to face whatever trials awaited them in the depths of the labyrinth's twisting corridors.

As the group emerged victorious from their battle with the Minotaur, they knew that their respite would be short-lived. For even as they caught their breath and tended to their wounds, the labyrinth seemed to come alive around them, its twisting corridors echoing with the sounds of battle as the army of monsters descended upon them once more.

With a fierce battle cry, Andrew rallied his comrades, his sword held high as he prepared to face their new adversaries head-on. Kiara stood at his side, her eyes blazing with determination as she summoned forth waves of water to engulf their foes. Adrian's mechanical traps sprang to life once more, ensnaring their enemies and buying precious moments of respite amidst the chaos of battle.

But despite their valiant efforts, the sheer number of monsters threatened to overwhelm them at every turn. For every creature they felled, two more seemed to take its place, their relentless advance pushing the group to their limits.

Yet still, they fought on with courage and determination that defied all odds. With Andrew's leadership guiding them and their bond of friendship as their strength, they pressed forward, their swords and spells cutting through the ranks of their enemies like a scythe through wheat.

But just when it seemed that all hope was lost, a blinding light filled the chamber, illuminating the darkness and scattering the monsters like leaves in the wind. With a triumphant cry, the group pressed their advantage, driving the remaining monsters back with renewed vigour and determination.

As the last of their foes fell before them, the group stood victorious amidst the wreckage of their fallen enemies, their chests heaving with exertion and their spirits uplifted by the knowledge that they had emerged triumphant once again. As they caught their breath and tended to their wounds, they knew that their journey through the labyrinth was far from over—but with their courage and determination as their guide, they were ready to face whatever challenges awaited them in the darkness that lay ahead.

With the echoes of battle still ringing in their ears, the group knew that they could not afford to rest for long. Though they had emerged victorious from their skirmish with the army of monsters, they were keenly aware that greater challenges awaited them in the depths of the labyrinth.

As they caught their breath and tended to their wounds, Andrew's mind raced with thoughts of their next move. They had come so far and faced countless trials and adversaries, but their quest was far from over. The Aegis still eluded them, its whereabouts shrouded in mystery, and the fate of both the mortal and immortal realms hung in the balance.

With a sense of purpose burning within him, Andrew rose to his feet, his gaze sweeping over his companions with a steely determination. "We must press on," he declared, his voice firm and resolute. "The Aegis awaits us, and we cannot afford to falter now."

His words were met with nods of agreement from his comrades, their eyes reflecting the same determination that burned within his own. With their bond of friendship as their guiding light, they knew that they could overcome any obstacle that stood in their way.

With renewed resolve, the group set out once more into the labyrinth's twisting corridors, their footsteps echoing off the ancient stone walls as they delved deeper into the darkness. Each step brought them closer to their goal, but also deeper into the heart of the labyrinth's mysteries.

As they ventured further into the labyrinth, the air grew colder, and the shadows seemed to lengthen around them. Strange whispers echoed through the corridors, and the sound of distant laughter filled their ears, sending shivers down their spines.

But still, they pressed on, their determination unyielding in the face of adversity. For they knew that the fate of both worlds depended on their success, and they would not rest until they had achieved their goal.

As they journeyed deeper into the labyrinth, they encountered new challenges and obstacles at every turn. Deadly traps lay in wait around every corner, and cunning puzzles tested their wits and ingenuity. But with their combined skills and teamwork, they overcame each challenge with ease, inching ever closer to their ultimate goal.

Yet amidst the darkness and danger, they also found moments of respite and camaraderie. They shared stories and laughter around campfires, their spirits buoyed by the knowledge that they were not alone in their struggles. And as they faced each new challenge together, they grew ever closer as friends and allies, bound by a shared purpose and a common destiny.

But as they ventured deeper into the labyrinth's depths, they could sense that they were drawing closer to the heart of the maze—and to the secrets that lay hidden within its ancient walls. For in the darkness that surrounded them, they knew that the Aegis awaited them, its power waiting to be unleashed upon the world.

With their courage and determination as their guide, they pressed on, ready to face whatever trials awaited them in the depths of the labyrinth's twisting corridors. For they knew that their quest was far from over and that the fate of both worlds depended on their success. With their bond of friendship as their strength, they would not rest until they had achieved their goal and emerged victorious from the darkness that threatened to consume them.

Top of Form

Chapter 7

BETRAYAL AND REDEMPTION

As the group ventured deeper into the labyrinth, their spirits buoyed by their recent victories, they could feel the weight of their quest pressing upon them like a heavy burden. With each step forward, they drew closer to their ultimate goal—the retrieval of the Aegis—but also closer to the heart of the labyrinth's mysteries.

Their journey had been fraught with danger and uncertainty, but they had faced each challenge with courage and determination, their bond of friendship serving as a beacon of hope in the darkness that surrounded them. Yet little did they know that their greatest trial lay just ahead, lurking in the shadows like a viper waiting to strike.

As they pressed on, their senses alert to the slightest hint of danger, Andrew couldn't shake the feeling of unease that gnawed at the edges of his mind. There was something amiss, a sense of foreboding that hung heavy in the air like a storm cloud on the horizon.

And then, without warning, disaster struck. As they rounded a corner in the labyrinth's twisting corridors, they found themselves face to face with an unexpected adversary—a figure cloaked in shadows, their features obscured by darkness.

At first, Andrew couldn't believe his eyes. The figure before them was none other than Marcus Fletcher, Harry's long-lost brother and the source of his deepest pain and sorrow. How could this be? Andrew wondered, his mind reeling with shock and disbelief.

But as Marcus stepped forward, his eyes gleaming with malice, Andrew realized the truth—he had been the traitor all along, lurking in their midst like a serpent waiting to strike. Betrayal burned in his gaze, a cold fire that sent shivers down Andrew's spine.

"We meet again, Andrew," Marcus sneered, his voice dripping with contempt. "I must say, I'm impressed by your persistence. But it seems that your luck has finally run out."

With a wave of his hand, Marcus summoned forth a horde of monsters, their eyes blazing with malevolence as they advanced upon the group with savage intent. Panic surged through Andrew's veins, his mind racing as he struggled to comprehend the enormity of their betrayal.

But even as fear threatened to consume him, Andrew knew that he could not falter. With his friends at his side, he stood firm, his sword held high as he prepared to face their treacherous foe head-on.

"Marcus, why?" Andrew demanded, his voice ringing out with righteous anger. "Why have you done this? What could possibly drive you to betray your own brother and aid our enemies?"

Marcus's laughter echoed through the chamber, a cruel sound that sent chills down Andrew's spine. "Oh, Andrew, you truly are naive," he sneered. "You think you know everything, but you know nothing of the true nature of power. The Aegis is mine by right, and I will stop at nothing to claim it."

With a cry of rage, Andrew lunged forward, his sword flashing in the dim light as he clashed with Marcus in a battle that would determine the fate of their quest. With each blow, he felt the weight of their betrayal pressing down upon him, driving him forward with a fierce determination that bordered on desperation.

But Marcus was no ordinary foe. With every move, he seemed to anticipate Andrew's attacks, his movements fluid and precise as he countered each blow with effortless grace. It was as if he had been preparing for this moment his entire life, his skills honed to perfection by years of training and discipline.

As the battle raged on, Andrew could feel his strength waning, his muscles burning with exertion as he struggled to keep pace with his adversary. But even as doubt threatened to overwhelm him, he knew that he could not give up—not now, not ever.

With a final, desperate effort, Andrew summoned forth every ounce of his courage and determination, channelling it into a single, decisive strike. With a mighty blow, he drove his sword deep into Marcus's chest, his heart pounding in his chest as he watched his foe fall to the ground, defeated at last.

But as Marcus lay dying at his feet, a sense of sadness washed over Andrew—a deep, profound sadness for what could have been, and what had been lost. For in the end, Marcus had been consumed by his own greed and ambition, his lust for power leading him down a path of darkness from which there could be no return.

And yet, even in death, there was redemption. As Marcus drew his final breath, a look of peace settled over his features, his eyes meeting Andrew's with a silent plea for forgiveness. And in that moment, Andrew knew that despite everything, Marcus had been his brother, and he would always carry a piece of him in his heart.

With a heavy heart, Andrew turned away from Marcus's lifeless form, his eyes meeting those of his friends with a mixture of sorrow and determination.

As the echoes of battle faded into the labyrinth's depths, the group stood in solemn silence, their hearts heavy with the weight of what had transpired. Marcus's betrayal had struck a deep blow, leaving them reeling with a sense of loss and betrayal. But amidst the darkness, a flicker of hope remained—the knowledge that they had overcome this trial together, their bond of friendship stronger than ever.

With a heavy sigh, Andrew turned to his companions, his gaze meeting theirs with a mixture of sorrow and determination. "We cannot afford to dwell on what has passed," he said, his voice steady despite the turmoil raging within him. "Our quest is far from over, and we must press on if we are to retrieve the Aegis and prevent it from falling into the wrong hands."

His words were met with nods of agreement from his friends, their resolve unshaken by the trials they had faced. With Marcus's betrayal still fresh in their minds, they knew that they could no longer afford to trust blindly. But they also knew that they had each other and that together, they were stronger than any obstacle that stood in their way.

With renewed determination, the group set out once more into the labyrinth's twisting corridors, their footsteps echoing off the ancient stone walls as they delved deeper into the darkness. Each step brought them closer to their ultimate goal, but also closer to the heart of the labyrinth's mysteries.

As they journeyed deeper into the labyrinth, they encountered new challenges and obstacles at every turn. Deadly traps lay in wait around every corner, and cunning puzzles tested their wits and ingenuity. But with their combined skills and teamwork, they overcame each challenge with ease, inching ever closer to their ultimate goal.

Yet amidst the darkness and danger, they also found moments of respite and camaraderie. They shared stories and laughter around campfires, their spirits buoyed by the knowledge that they were not alone in their struggles. And as they faced each new challenge together, they grew ever closer as friends and allies, bound by a shared purpose and a common destiny.

But as they ventured deeper into the labyrinth's depths, they could sense that they were drawing closer to the heart of the maze—and to the secrets that lay hidden within its ancient walls. For in the darkness that surrounded them, they knew that the Aegis awaited them, its power waiting to be unleashed upon the world.

With their courage and determination as their guide, they pressed on, ready to face whatever trials awaited them in the depths of the labyrinth's twisting corridors. For they knew that their quest was far from over and that the fate of both worlds depended on their success. With their bond of friendship as their strength, they would not rest until they had achieved their goal and emerged victorious from the darkness that threatened to consume them.

Chapter 8

AEGIS REVEALED

After navigating through the labyrinth's treacherous corridors and overcoming countless obstacles, the group finally reached the chamber where the Aegis was hidden. The air crackled with magical energy, and a sense of anticipation hung heavy in the air as they prepared to confront whatever challenges lay ahead.

With Adrian's keen knowledge of mechanics and Harry's connection to the underworld, they knew that they had the skills and abilities needed to unlock the chamber and retrieve the artefact. But they also knew that their victory was far from assured, for powerful magic guarded the Aegis, and they would have to tread carefully if they were to succeed.

With a nod of determination, Andrew turned to his companions, his eyes meeting theirs with a silent understanding. "This is it," he said, his voice filled with quiet resolve. "We've come too far to turn back now. Whatever awaits us in that chamber, we face it together."

His words were met with nods of agreement from his friends, their resolve unshaken by the challenges that lay ahead. With their bond of friendship as their guiding light, they stepped forward as one, ready to confront whatever trials awaited them in the depths of the chamber.

As they entered the chamber, they were greeted by a sight that took their breath away—a vast expanse of glittering treasures and ancient artefacts, each one more wondrous than the last. But amidst the splendour, their eyes were drawn to a pedestal at the centre of the chamber, upon which rested the Aegis, its surface shimmering with otherworldly energy.

With bated breath, they approached the pedestal, their hearts pounding with anticipation as they reached out to claim the artefact. But as their hands closed around the Aegis, they felt a surge of power ripple through their bodies, and they knew that they had unlocked its secrets at last.

With Adrian and Harry working together to decipher the ancient runes that adorned the Aegis, they unlocked its full potential, tapping into its power to shield themselves from harm and unlock the chamber's secrets. With each twist and turn of the mechanisms, they felt the magic of the Aegis grow stronger, its energy pulsing through their veins like a living force.

But their victory was short-lived, for even as they basked in the glow of their success, they were ambushed by an unexpected foe—a figure cloaked in shadows, their features obscured by darkness. With a cry of alarm, the group sprang into action, their weapons at the ready as they prepared to face their mysterious assailant.

As the figure emerged from the shadows, their identity was revealed—a powerful sorcerer, his eyes burning with malice as he prepared to unleash his dark magic upon them. With a wave of his hand, he summoned forth a horde of shadowy creatures, their twisted forms twisting and writhing with unnatural energy as they advanced upon the group with savage intent.

With their backs against the wall and nowhere to run, the group knew that they would have to fight for their lives if they were to survive. With Andrew leading the charge, they clashed with their mysterious assailant and his shadowy minions, their weapons flashing in the dim light as they battled against overwhelming odds.

But even as they fought with all their might, they could feel the tide of battle turning against them. The sorcerer's dark magic was too powerful, his minions too numerous, and they soon found themselves overwhelmed by the sheer force of their enemies onslaught.

With every blow, they felt their strength waning, their resolve faltering as they struggled to hold their ground against the relentless assault. But even in the face of despair, they refused to give up—not now, not ever.

With a cry of defiance, Andrew rallied his comrades, his voice ringing out with unwavering determination as he urged them to stand firm against their enemies. With their bond of friendship as their shield and their courage as their sword, they fought on with a ferocity born of desperation, their hearts filled with the hope that they would emerge victorious from the darkness that threatened to consume them.

And as they clashed with their enemies with all the strength and skill they possessed, they knew that their victory was not assured. But they also knew that they would never surrender, not as long as they had each other and the indomitable spirit of defiance that burned within their hearts. For they were not just a group of friends—they were warriors, bound together by a common purpose and a shared destiny, ready to face whatever challenges lay ahead in the eternal struggle between light and darkness.

As the battle raged on, the chamber echoed with the clash of steel and the crackle of dark magic, the air thick with tension as the group fought desperately to overcome their foes. Andrew's sword flashed in the dim light, his movements fluid and precise as he engaged the sorcerer in a deadly dance of blades.

Beside him, Kiara summoned torrents of water to engulf their enemies, her mastery of the sea proved to be a formidable weapon against their shadowy assailants. With each wave she unleashed, the creatures faltered, their forms dissolving into nothingness as they were swept away by the tide.

Meanwhile, Adrian and Harry worked together to devise a plan to turn the tide of battle in their favour. Drawing upon their respective skills and knowledge, they unleashed a barrage of traps and gadgets, each one designed to confound and confuse their enemies.

But despite their best efforts, the sorcerer's dark magic proved to be a formidable adversary, his power seemingly limitless as he unleashed wave after wave of shadowy minions to assail the group. With every blow, they felt their strength waning, their resolve faltering as they struggled to hold their ground against the relentless onslaught.

But even in the face of overwhelming odds, they refused to surrender. With their bond of friendship as their shield and their courage as their sword, they fought on with a ferocity born of desperation, their hearts filled with the hope that they would emerge victorious from the darkness that threatened to consume them.

And then, just when all seemed lost, a glimmer of hope appeared on the horizon—a ray of light amidst the darkness that surrounded them. With a cry of triumph, Andrew and his friends rallied together, their spirits renewed as they unleashed a final, devastating assault upon their enemies.

With a mighty roar, they charged forward as one, their weapons flashing in the dim light as they struck with all their might against their foes. As the sorcerer's dark magic faltered and failed, the chamber erupted into chaos, the echoes of battle filling the air as the group fought tooth and nail for their very survival.

But amidst the chaos and carnage, a single figure stood resolute—the sorcerer, his eyes burning with hatred as he prepared to unleash one final, devastating attack. With a wave of his hand, he summoned forth a vortex of dark energy, its tendrils reaching out to ensnare the group in its deadly embrace.

As the sorcerer's dark magic surged around them, threatening to engulf Andrew and his companions, Harry's eyes narrowed with determination. With a primal roar, he tapped into the depths of his power, channelling the shadows that lay dormant within him into a focused torrent of energy.

With a swift motion, Harry unleashed the full force of his power, sending a concentrated blast of shadowy energy hurtling towards the sorcerer. The dark tendrils coiled and writhed as they closed in on their target, enveloping the sorcerer in a suffocating embrace.

With a strangled cry, the sorcerer struggled against the darkness that threatened to consume him, his form writhing and contorting as he fought to break free. But Harry's grip was unrelenting, his power fueled by a sense of righteous fury as he unleashed wave after wave of shadowy energy upon his foe.

With each blast, the sorcerer's strength waned, his once formidable defences crumbling under the relentless assault. Desperation flashed in his eyes as he realized the futility of his struggle, his dark magic flickering and fading like a dying flame.

And then, with one final surge of power, Harry unleashed a torrent of shadows that surged forward like a tidal wave, engulfing the sorcerer in its dark embrace. With a primal scream, the sorcerer collapsed to his knees, his form trembling with the effort to maintain his control over the swirling vortex of magic that surrounded him.

As the defeated sorcerer lay sprawled on the chamber floor, his breaths laboured and eyes filled with a mix of defiance and resignation, Andrew cautiously approached him. With a wary glance at his companions, Andrew knelt beside the fallen foe, his grip tight on his sword, ready to defend against any last desperate attempt at retaliation.

"What... do you want?" the sorcerer managed to rasp, his voice strained and hoarse.

"We seek the Aegis," Andrew replied evenly, his tone unwavering. "And we will retrieve it, one way or another."

The sorcerer's lips curled into a bitter smirk, his gaze locking with Andrew's. "You fools," he spat, his voice thick with venom. "You have no idea what you're dealing with. The Aegis is but a trinket compared to the power that now rises."

Andrew's brows furrowed in suspicion, but before he could press the sorcerer for answers, the air around them seemed to shimmer with dark energy. With a sudden flash, the sorcerer produced a twisted amulet from the depths of his robes, its surface pulsing with malevolent energy.

"Take this," the sorcerer hissed, thrusting the amulet toward Andrew. "It will lead you to the one you seek—the true enemy of gods and mortals alike."

Andrew hesitated, eyeing the amulet warily. But a sense of urgency gnawed at his insides, urging him to seize the opportunity before him. With a cautious nod, he reached out and accepted the amulet, feeling its dark power thrumming beneath his fingertips.

Before Andrew could question the sorcerer further, a sudden blast of energy enveloped the chamber, blinding him momentarily. When the light faded, the sorcerer was gone, leaving behind only an ominous sense of foreboding.

With the Aegis in hand and the sorcerer's warning echoing in their minds, Andrew and his companions wasted no time in making their escape from the chamber. As they emerged into the cool night air, the weight of their newfound knowledge hung heavy upon them.

But amidst the darkness and uncertainty, they knew that their mission was far from over. With the Aegis as their shield and the sorcerer's warning as their guide, they would confront the true enemy that now threatened to engulf both gods and mortals in its shadowy embrace.

With a solemn nod to his companions, Andrew set his jaw with determination. Their journey was far from over, and the fate of the world now rested squarely on their shoulders. But with their bond of friendship as their strength, they would face whatever challenges lay ahead, ready to confront the darkness and emerge victorious once more.

With the Aegis secured and the knowledge of a greater evil looming over them, Andrew and his companions knew that they could not face this threat alone. As they made their way out of the chamber and back into the cool night air, they exchanged grim glances, the weight of their newfound burden heavy upon their shoulders.

"We need to go to Camp Half-Blood," Andrew declared, his voice firm with resolve. "We must rally an army if we are to stand any chance against this new threat."

His companions nodded in agreement, their expressions reflecting the gravity of the situation. They knew that the safety of both mortal and immortal realms hung in the balance and that they would need all the help they could get to confront the looming darkness.

With a shared sense of purpose, they set out towards Camp Half-Blood, their footsteps quickening with each passing moment. Along the way, they discussed their plan of action, strategizing on how best to rally the demigods to their cause.

"We'll need to speak to Chiron first," Kiara suggested, her voice steady despite the uncertainty that clouded their path. "He'll know how to best approach the situation and gather support."

Andrew nodded in agreement, his mind already racing with thoughts of the battles that lay ahead. "Once we have Chiron's support, we can begin reaching out to the other campers," he said, his tone resolute. "We must unite them under a common cause if we are to stand any chance against this new enemy."

Chapter 9

DARKNESS UNVEILED

As the weary travellers finally crossed the threshold of Camp Half-Blood, a collective sigh of relief echoed through the air. The camp greeted them with open arms, the familiar sights and sounds offering a comforting embrace after their arduous journey. Chiron, the wise centaur who served as mentor and guardian to the campers, approached them with a concerned furrow in his brow, his eyes filled with a mixture of relief and apprehension.

"It is good to see you return safely," Chiron greeted them, his voice warm but tinged with worry. "But I fear that your journey is not yet over."

Andrew nodded solemnly, his gaze meeting Chiron's with a sense of resolve. "We have faced many trials and challenges," he began, his voice steady despite the weight of their mission. "But our greatest battle lies ahead."

As Andrew recounted their encounter with the sorcerer and the dire warning he had given them, a sombre silence fell over the camp. The gravity of their situation hung heavy in the air, each word spoken by Andrew serving as a stark reminder of the peril that awaited them.

But just as Andrew finished speaking, a figure emerged from the shadows, her presence commanding the attention of all who stood before her. It was Athena, the goddess of wisdom and strategy, her eyes shining with an otherworldly light as she surveyed the gathered campers.

"You have faced a great challenge," Athena spoke, her voice carrying with it the weight of centuries of knowledge and experience. "But the true battle lies ahead."

Andrew's heart skipped a beat at her words, the enormity of their task weighing heavily upon him. But before he could respond, Athena continued.

"The sorcerer you faced was but a pawn in a much larger game," she explained, her voice filled with a sense of urgency. "A greater evil has risen—one that threatens to tear Olympus itself asunder."

As murmurs of disbelief and concern rippled through the crowd, Athena's gaze fell upon Andrew, her eyes piercing and wise. "You have proven yourself to be a capable leader and a true hero, Andrew Lancaster," she said. "But this is a task that cannot be faced alone. You must come to Olympus and plead your case before the gods themselves."

Andrew's breath caught in his throat at her words, the weight of her request settling like a stone in his chest. But before he could respond, Athena added one final decree.

"However," she said, her voice firm but compassionate, "you will not journey alone. Your companions have proven themselves worthy allies, and they too shall accompany you to Olympus."

A wave of relief washed over Andrew as he turned to his friends, gratitude shining in his eyes. For in that moment, he knew that no matter what trials lay ahead, they would face them together, united in their quest to save both mortal and immortal realms from the darkness that threatened to engulf them all.

As Athena's words hung in the air, a shimmering light enveloped Andrew and his companions, lifting them from the familiar grounds of Camp Half-Blood and transporting them to the majestic heights of Mount Olympus.

The transition was breathtaking, the mortal world falling away beneath them as they ascended to the realm of the gods. The air grew thinner, tinged with the heady scent of ambrosia and the distant echoes of celestial music.

As they emerged into the grandeur of Olympus, Andrew and his companions found themselves standing before the throne room, its marble pillars reaching towards the heavens and its golden doors adorned with intricate carvings of myth and legend.

Before them sat the gods of Olympus, their forms radiant and awe-inspiring as they regarded the mortals who stood before them. Zeus, king of the gods, sat upon his throne, his gaze stern but curious as he listened to Andrew's tale unfold.

With a deep breath, Andrew stepped forward, his voice steady despite the weight of the task that lay before him. He recounted their encounter with the sorcerer and the dire warning he had given them, his words painting a vivid picture of the darkness that threatened to engulf both mortal and immortal realms alike.

As he spoke, the gods listened in rapt attention, their expressions ranging from solemn contemplation to righteous fury. Hera, queen of the gods, clutched the arm of her throne, her eyes flashing with indignation at the thought of such a threat to her domain.

But it was Athena who listened most intently, her eyes locked with Andrew's as he spoke of their journey and the trials they had faced. She nodded in understanding, her expression a mixture of pride and concern as she regarded the mortal hero who stood before her.

When Andrew had finished speaking, there was a moment of silence, the weight of his words hanging heavy in the air. And then, Zeus spoke, his voice echoing throughout the throne room with the authority of thunder.

"We have heard your tale, Andrew Lancaster," he boomed, his voice commanding the attention of all who stood before him. "And we shall take heed of your warning."

With a wave of his hand, Zeus motioned for the Aegis to be brought forward, its shimmering surface reflecting the light of Olympus with an otherworldly glow. Andrew stepped forward, presenting the artefact to the gods with reverence and respect.

As the gods regarded the Aegis with a mixture of awe and reverence, Athena spoke once more, her voice filled with determination. "We shall stand united against this new threat," she declared, her eyes shining with the fire of battle. "And together, we shall vanquish the darkness that threatens to engulf us all."

As the council of gods convened on Mount Olympus, Apollo, the god of prophecy and music, rose from his seat, his golden lyre glinting in the divine light. With a solemn expression, he addressed the gathered assembly, his voice carrying the weight of the ages.

"My fellow gods and goddesses," Apollo began, his tone grave and measured. "I have received a new prophecy—a vision of darkness that threatens to engulf both mortal and immortal realms alike."

As Apollo's voice resonated through the halls of Olympus, the prophecy he unveiled echoed with a weight that sent shivers down the spines of both gods and mortals alike. Each line was imbued with a sense of urgency, a foreboding reminder of the trials that lay ahead.

"Athena's mind, Hades' touch so grim, Poseidon's fury, Hephaestus' limb, Four heroes destined, a pact they will make, Forged in the depths, the world's fate to take."

The words hung in the air, their meaning reverberating through the throne room with an intensity that left no doubt as to their significance. Athena's mind, sharp and strategic, Hades' touch, foreboding and mysterious, Poseidon's fury, vast and uncontrollable, Hephaestus' limb, skilled and precise—all four elements of the prophecy spoke of power and purpose, of destinies and fates entwined.

For Andrew and his companions, the prophecy held both promise and peril. They were the chosen ones, the heroes destined to confront the darkness that threatened to consume both mortal and immortal realms. But with that destiny came great responsibility, and they knew that they could not face the challenges ahead alone.

With a shared glance, Andrew and his companions nodded in silent agreement, their resolve hardened by the weight of the prophecy they had been entrusted with. Together, they would forge a pact—a bond that would withstand the trials to come and lead them to victory against the encroaching evil.

For in the depths of their souls, they knew that their fate was intertwined with the fate of the world itself. And as they stood united before the gods of Olympus, they vowed to fulfil their destiny, no matter the cost, for they were the heroes foretold by prophecy, and their journey had only just begun.

As the moon rose high in the night sky, casting its silvery glow over the sacred grounds of Camp Half-Blood, Andrew approached Chiron with a sense of purpose burning in his heart. The camp was quiet, the air heavy with anticipation as Andrew recounted the events that had transpired on Mount Olympus—the revelation of Kronos' return, the urgency of their mission, and the need to gather an army to stand against the encroaching darkness.

Chiron listened intently, his wise eyes reflecting the gravity of the situation. As Andrew finished speaking, a solemn silence settled over the camp, each camper grappling with the enormity of the task that lay ahead.

But amidst the uncertainty, there was a glimmer of hope—a determination to stand united against the forces of darkness and to fight for the future of both mortal and immortal realms.

To be continued......

Don't miss out!

Visit the website below and you can sign up to receive emails whenever Tharun Vigneswar PS publishes a new book. There's no charge and no obligation.

https://books2read.com/r/B-A-LBUIB-TURDD

BOOKS 2 READ

Connecting independent readers to independent writers.

Also by Tharun Vigneswar PS

Andrew Lancaster and The Olympians
Darkness Rising
Legacy of Darkness

Milton Keynes UK
Ingram Content Group UK Ltd.
UKHW010748110624
444053UK00001B/48